The Berenstain Bears

SAFE and SOUND!

"Better safe than sorry!"
says wise Mama Bear.
Let's follow her rule
and be careful out there!

The Berenstain Bears

SAFE and SOUND!

Jan & Mike Berenstain

HarperFestival®

A Division of HarperCollinsPublishers

The Berenstain Bears: Safe and Sound!
Copyright © 2009 by Berenstain Bears, Inc.
HarperCollins®, ≜®, and HarperFestival® are trademarks of HarperCollins Publishers.
All rights reserved. Manufactured in China.
No part of this book may be used or reproduced in any manner whatsoever without written permission except in the case of brief quotations embodied in critical articles and reviews.
For information address HarperCollins Children's Books, a division of HarperCollins Publishers, 10 East 53rd Street, New York, NY 10022.
Library of Congress catalog card number is available.
ISBN 978-0-06-057407-9 (trade bdg.)—ISBN 978-0-06-057391-1 (pbk.)
www.harpercollinschildrens.com
12 13 14 SCP 10 9 8 7 6 5 4 3
❖
First Edition

Brother and Sister Bear didn't like to just sit around all day. They liked to go outside and *do* things. One bright Saturday afternoon, they ran outside after lunch and hopped on their trusty skateboards. They took off down the driveway, heading for the schoolyard.

"Just a minute!" called Mama, running after them. "Aren't you two forgetting something?" She held up their safety helmets, knee pads, and elbow and wrist guards.

"Oh, Mama!" said Brother. "Do we really need those? We're just going down to the schoolyard for a while."

"Be that as it may," said Mama, planting the helmets firmly on their heads, "better safe than sorry!"

"But Mama," complained Sister, "these pads and helmets are hot and heavy."

"If you want to go skateboarding," said Mama, crossing her arms, "you're going to wear your safety gear."

Brother and Sister knew better than to argue with Mama when her arms were crossed.

"Okay, Mama!" They both sighed, hopping back on their boards and heading down the road at top speed to make up for lost time.

But when they arrived at the schoolyard, instead of finding it full of cubs zipping around on their skateboards, they saw a crowd gathered around a big sign.

NO SKATEBOARDING ALLOWED ON WEEKENDS
By order of Mr. Honeycomb, Principal

Bear Country Sch

The sign said:

NO SKATEBOARDING
ALLOWED ON WEEKENDS

By order of Mr. Honeycomb, Principal

"Oh, no!" said Cousin Fred. "Why aren't we allowed to skateboard here anymore?"

"Mr. Honeycomb said it's too dangerous to skateboard when the teachers aren't on duty to keep an eye on us," said Queenie McBear, who was always in the know.

Disgusted, the cubs picked up their skateboards and headed for home. Sister and Brother trudged along taking turns kicking a tin can down the road.

Brother groaned. "What are we going to do now?"

"I dunno!" said Sister. "Do something else, I guess."

"Like what?" said Brother.

Before they could figure out a new plan, Too-Tall
Grizzly and his gang stepped out from behind the bushes.
"Why are you goody-two-shoes moping around?" He
sneered. "Are you late for ballet class?" The rest of the
gang laughed.

Brother and Sister were too gloomy to get angry. "No, Too-Tall," explained Brother. "They closed the schoolyard for skateboarding. Now we've got nowhere to skateboard on weekends."

"No problem!" Too-Tall grinned. "*We've* got a place to skateboard."

Brother and Sister brightened up. "Really?" they said. "Where?"
"Our own private skate park," said Too-Tall, putting his arm around
Brother's shoulders. "Just step this way!"

Too-Tall's skate park was jammed in among the tree trunks.

"We built this ourselves," said Too-Tall. "We've got the works—jumps and ramps, rails and half pipes."

"Wow!" said Brother. "This is great!"

"Go ahead and try it out," said Too-Tall. "We've got just one rule—no safety gear allowed."

"What?" said Brother and Sister, startled.

That's right," said Too-Tall. "Safety is for sissies!"

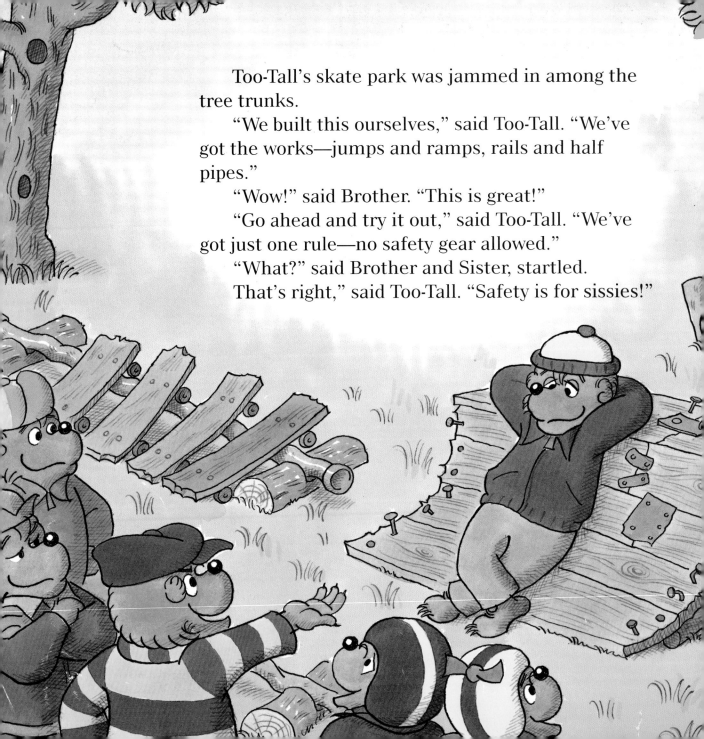

Too-Tall and the gang got on their homemade skateboards and hit the ramps. Brother and Sister hesitated. They could almost hear Mama saying, "Better safe than sorry!" But Too-Tall was entitled to make his own rules. It didn't take them long to drop their helmets and pads quietly in the bushes.

"WHOOPEE!" yelled Brother as he zoomed off a hollow-tree half pipe.

"GERONIMO!" shouted Sister, doing a "grab" as she shot up from an old stump ramp.

Then Too-Tall lost his balance on a twisty branch rail and went flying head over heels into a sticker bush. *KER-FLUMP!* The gang all took a break to dig him out.

"How many fingers can you see?" asked Brother, holding three fingers in front of Too-Tall's nose.

"Uh . . . twelve?" guessed Too-Tall, his eyes rolling around.

"Maybe you should take a break, Too-Tall," said Sister.

"Nah!" He laughed. "I'm fine! Come on, you guys, back to the ramps!"

Brother and Sister watched Too-Tall trying to get on his skateboard. He wasn't having much success.

"Hmm!" they both said. Maybe it was better to be safe than sorry after all.

Brother and Sister picked up their safety gear and sneaked out of the woods while Too-Tall and the gang were bouncing off the trees.

But they still had no place to skateboard. When they got home, they were down in the dumps.

"What's wrong?" Papa asked. "Why are you back so soon?"

Brother explained about the schoolyard being closed to skateboarding.

"So where are you going to skateboard now?" asked Papa.

"No place," said Brother. "Too-Tall has a skate park in the woods. But he won't let us wear our safety gear and, well, we don't think that's such a good idea."

"Smart thinking!" said Papa, impressed.

"Now, I think I know how to solve this little problem." He went into his workshop and brought out some sheets of plywood. "These ought to work," he said.

"What are you going to do?" asked Brother and Sister.

"*We* are going to build our very own skate park!" said Papa, grabbing his tools.

"YAY!" cried Sister and Brother, jumping up and down in excitement.

Papa asked Farmer Ben if they could build the skate park in his unused back pasture. Farmer Ben thought it was a fine idea.

Papa, Mama, Brother, Sister, and even little Honey all set to work. Brother and Sister were the designers, Papa was the carpenter, and Mama and Honey were the painters.

Word of the Bear family's skate park project got around the neighborhood, and before long other bears showed up to help out.

Soon Farmer Ben, Grizzly Gus, Officer Marguerite, Teacher Bob, and even Principal Honeycomb were down in the back pasture helping to build the skate park. Farmer Ben's cows had a ringside seat.

When the park was finished, it was decided that it would be the official Bear Country Skate Park. Mayor Honeypot, himself, came to the opening and gave a speech. He was almost knocked over by the rush of cubs trying to get in. Even Too-Tall and his gang showed up.

But the Bear Country Skate Park had just one rule: "Safety gear must be worn at all times"—even by Too-Tall Grizzly!

"Like I always say," Too-Tall said, "better safe than sorry!"